CHILDREN'S THRIFT CLASSICS

The Three
Billy Goats Gruff
and Other
Read-Aloud Stories

EDITED BY CAROLYN SHERWIN BAILEY

Illustrated by Thea Kliros

DOVER PUBLICATIONS, INC.
New York

DOVER CHILDREN'S THRIFT CLASSICS
EDITOR OF THIS VOLUME: CANDACE WARD

Copyright

Bibliographical Note

The Three Billy Goats Gruff and Other Read-Aloud Stories is a new selection of unabridged stories from *Firelight Stories: Folk Tales Retold for Kindergarten, School and Home*, first published by Milton Bradley Company, Springfield, Massachusetts, in 1907. The illustrations and an introductory note have been specially prepared for this edition.

Library of Congress Cataloging-in-Publication Data

The Three billy goats Gruff and other read-aloud stories / edited by Carolyn Sherwin Bailey.
      p.   cm.—(Dover children's thrift stories)
  "A new selection of unabridged stories from Firelight stories . . . 1907"—T.p. verso.
  Summary: Presents a collection of twenty–two folk tales from around the world, including "The Teeny, Tiny Lady," "The Wonderful Pot," and "Why the Field Mouse Is Little."
  ISBN 0-486-28021-7 (pbk.)
  1. Tales. [1. Folklore.] I. Bailey, Carolyn Sherwin, 1875–1961. II. Bailey, Carolyn Sherwin, 1875–1961. Firelight stories. Selections. 1994. III. Title: 3 billy goats Gruff and other read-aloud stories. IV. Series.
PZ8.1.T382   1994
398.2—dc20
[E]   93-33492
                                                      CIP
                                                       AC

Manufactured in the United States by Courier Corporation
28021706
www.doverpublications.com

Note

CAROLYN SHERWIN BAILEY (1875–1961) was a prolific American author and editor of children's books. For many years she was the editor of *American Childhood* magazine, and in 1947 she won the Newbery Medal for her doll story, *Miss Hickory*.

The twenty-two stories in this edition were selected from Bailey's *Firelight Stories*, a compilation of folk tales from around the world. As with much folklore, the stories' use of rhyme and repetition reflects their roots in oral traditions and most of these stories appear in various forms in different countries. "Johnny Cake," for example, appears in Grimm as "The Pancake" and in other English-speaking countries as "The Gingerbread Man." "The Wonderful Pot," a Danish tale, also appears in varying form in Grimm, and "How the Fox Played Herdsman," "Why the Bear Has a Stumpy Tail" and "The Three Billy Goats Gruff" are Norwegian folk tales. From Southern black culture comes "Why the Bear Sleeps All Winter" and "Little Bear," both of which were among the stories still being told in Georgia and the Carolinas when Bailey was working on her collection. Whatever the origin of these classic tales, children of all backgrounds will enjoy hearing them read aloud as well as reading them on their own.

Contents

List of Illustrations

iv

The Three Billy Goats Gruff

ONCE UPON A TIME there were three Billy Goats, and one was a very large Goat, and one was a middle-sized Goat, and one was a tiny Goat, but the three had the very same name, which was Gruff.

One morning the three Billy Goats started away from home, for they had decided to go far, far to a hillside where there was a quantity of green grass, and they might eat of it and make themselves fat.

Now, on the way to the hillside there ran a brook, and over the brook was a bridge, and under the bridge lived a Troll with eyes as large as saucers, and a nose as long as a poker. And this Troll was fond of eating Billy Goats.

First of all came the youngest Billy Goat Gruff to cross over the bridge. Trip trap, trip trap, his little feet pattered upon the boards.

"Who is that tripping over my bridge?" called up the Troll in a surly voice.

"Oh, it's only I, the tiniest Billy Goat Gruff, going over to the hillside to make myself fat," the Goat called back in a wee, small voice.

"I am coming to gobble you up, Billy Goat Gruff," said the Troll.

"Oh, no, pray do not take me," said the tiniest Billy Goat Gruff; "I am too little, that I am. Wait until the second Billy Goat Gruff comes along. He is ever so much bigger than I."

"Well, be off with you," said the Troll.

Then came the middle-sized Billy Goat Gruff, to cross the bridge. Trip trap, trip trap, his middle-sized feet pattered upon the boards.

"Who is that tripping over my bridge?" called up the Troll.

"Oh, it's only I, the middle-sized Billy Goat Gruff, going over to the hillside to make myself fat," the Goat called back in a middle-sized voice.

"I am coming to gobble you up, Billy Goat Gruff," said the Troll.

"Oh, no, pray do not take me," said the middle-sized Billy Goat Gruff; "I am a little larger than the tiniest Billy Goat, but I am not large enough to make a mouthful for you. Of that I am quite sure."

"Well, be off with you," said the Troll.

The Goat tossed the Troll so high with his horns that no
one has ever seen a Troll under a bridge
from that day to this.

Then, last of all, came the great Billy Goat Gruff, to cross over the bridge.

Trip trap, trip trap, his great feet tramped across the boards.

"Who is that tramping over my bridge?" called up the Troll.

"It is I, the great Billy Goat Gruff, going over to the hillside to make myself fat," the Goat called back in a great voice.

"I am coming to gobble you up, Billy Goat Gruff," said the Troll.

"Come along," said the great Billy Goat Gruff.

So the Troll, whose eyes were large as saucers and his nose as long as a poker, came hurrying up to the top of the bridge,—but, ah, this is what happened to him.

There on the bridge stood the great Billy Goat Gruff with his feet firmly planted on the boards and his head lowered, and so soon as the Troll came near—rush, scamper—the Goat tossed the Troll so high with his horns that no one has ever seen a Troll under a bridge from that day to this.

Then the great Billy Goat Gruff went on to the hillside, and the three Billy Goats ate, and ate, and made themselves so fat that they could scarcely walk home again.

The Teeny, Tiny Lady

ONCE UPON A TIME there was a teeny, tiny lady who lived in a teeny, tiny house in a teeny, tiny village.

One day this teeny, tiny lady put on her teeny, tiny bonnet, and tied the teeny, tiny strings under her teeny, tiny chin, for she thought she would go for a teeny, tiny walk.

So she walked, and walked, and she came to a teeny, tiny gate which led into a teeny, tiny field. The teeny, tiny lady opened the gate, and walked into the field, and there, at the foot of a teeny, tiny tree, sat a teeny, tiny hen.

"This teeny, tiny hen will lay me a teeny, tiny egg for my teeny, tiny breakfast," said the teeny, tiny lady; so she took the teeny, tiny hen, and put it in her teeny, tiny reticule, and she went home again.

But when she came to her teeny, tiny house, she felt a teeny, tiny tired, so she put the teeny, tiny hen in her teeny, tiny cupboard, and she went upstairs to take a teeny, tiny nap.

And she had not been asleep so very long when she heard a teeny, tiny voice which woke her, and it said:—

"Give me my hen."

Then the teeny, tiny lady was a teeny, tiny afraid, but she pulled the teeny, tiny quilt up to her teeny, tiny chin and she went to sleep again.

But soon she heard the teeny, tiny voice again, and it said a little louder:—

"Give me my hen!"

Then the teeny, tiny lady was a teeny, tiny more afraid, but she hid her teeny, tiny head in her teeny, tiny quilt, and she went to sleep again.

But very soon the voice called again, very loud:—

"GIVE ME MY HEN!"

Then the teeny, tiny lady sat up in bed, and she called out in a loud teeny, tiny voice:—

"TAKE IT!"

And when it came morning, the teeny, tiny lady went down stairs, and looked in her teeny, tiny cupboard; and what do you think? The teeny, tiny hen was *gone!*

The Wee, Wee Man

ONCE UPON A TIME, when all the big folks were wee folks, and it is so long a time since that you could never count the years, there lived a wee, wee man, and he had a huge, huge cow.

One morning very early out went the wee, wee man to milk his huge, huge cow, and to her he said:—

> "Hold still, my cow, my pretty,
> Hold still, my pretty, my cow,
> And you shall have for dinner
> A cake of milk white dough."

But the huge, huge cow would not stand still. She jumped and she danced and she kicked, tipping over the milking stool and spilling all the milk.

So the wee, wee man cried out in a loud voice:—

> "Hold still, my cow, my dearie,
> And fill my bucket with milk,

7

> And if you are not contrary,
> I'll give you a gown of silk."

But the huge, huge cow would not stand still.

"Now, look at that," said the wee, wee man.

> "What is a wee, wee man to do,
> With such a huge, huge cow as you?"

Then off he went to his grandmother's house, and to his grandmother he said:—

"Cow will not stand still. Wee, wee man cannot milk her."

"Take a stick and shake it at her," said his grandmother. So off went the wee, wee man to the hazel tree for a stick, and to the tree he said:—

> "Break, stick, break,
> And I'll give you a cake."

But the stick would not break, and the wee, wee man went back to his grandmother's house, saying:—

"Grandmother, grandmother, stick will not break: huge, huge cow will not stand still: wee, wee man cannot milk her."

"Then go to the butcher and bid him tie the cow," said his grandmother.

So off went the wee, wee man to the Butcher, and to the Butcher he said:—

"Butcher, tie the huge, huge cow.
She is good for naught for she dances now."

But the Butcher was just sweeping his shop, and he would not tie the cow, so the wee, wee man went back to his grandmother's house, saying:—

"Grandmother, grandmother, Butcher will not come. Stick will not break. Huge, huge cow will not stand still. Wee, wee man cannot milk her. What is wee, wee man to do?"

"I know not," said his grandmother, but just then along came a little girl with a cup in her hand.

"Please give me milk to make a cake," said the little girl, "my mother would bake to-day."

"Run," said the grandmother to the wee, wee man, "tell the huge, huge cow there's a pretty little lady with long yellow hair waiting for a cup of milk."

So the wee, wee man ran as fast as his wee, wee legs would carry him, and he said to the cow:—

"You'll not stand for the cake or the gown of silk.
Will you give pretty lady a cup of milk?"

"MOO, MOO," said the huge, huge cow in a huge, huge voice, "that I will."

So she stood very still, and neither jumped, nor danced, nor kicked over the milking stool; and that is how the wee, wee man milked his huge, huge cow after all.

Mrs. Vinegar."

So Mr. Vinegar, with a bright, shining face,
traveled all the rest of the night to find a
house that he could buy for one gold piece.

days," thought Mr. Vinegar, as he

piece. Mr. Vinegar's feet bega

But after Mr. Vinegar had

made no noise. Then along came a man

Mr. and Mrs. Vinegar

ONCE UPON A TIME Mr. and Mrs. Vinegar
lived in a fine, large bottle. But one day
Mrs. Vinegar swept her house so hard with
her little broom that the bottle broke to bits.

"Oh, Mr. Vinegar, Mr. Vinegar!" cried Mrs.
Vinegar, "our house is broken to bits. What
shall we do?"

"We will find a new house, my dear," said
Mr. Vinegar. So he put the door, which was not
broken, on his back, and they started off to
find a new house.

They traveled all day, but they found no
new house, so at night they climbed up in a
tree to sleep until morning. They had just
gone to sleep when some one at the foot of
the tree called out so loudly that they both
awoke at once.

"Robbers, my dear," cried Mr. Vinegar. "I
will climb down the tree and frighten them
away."

So Mr. Vinegar climbed down the tree and

11

frightened away the robbers. And as the robbers ran, they dropped a gold piece.

"I will buy a house with this gold piece," said Mr. Vinegar, picking it up, "and surprise Mrs. Vinegar."

So Mr. Vinegar, who was a foolish little man, traveled all the rest of the night to find a house that he could buy for one gold piece, and there was none.

When it came morning he met a farmer driving a red cow. Mr. Vinegar forgot all about the house, and he bought the red cow from the farmer for the gold piece.

"She will give us milk for the rest of our days," thought Mr. Vinegar, as he drove the red cow merrily along.

But soon he heard some music in the road ahead of him. It was a man playing the bagpipes. Mr. Vinegar's feet began to dance, and he hurried up to the man.

"Will you sell your bagpipes for this red cow, sir?" asked Mr. Vinegar.

"That I will," said the man, and he took the red cow.

But after Mr. Vinegar had bought the bagpipes he could not play them. He sat down by the roadside, and he blew and he blew, but he made no music. Then along came a man wearing some fine fur gloves.

"Will you give me those gloves for my bag-pipes, sir?" he asked the man.

"That I will," said the man, and he took the bagpipes, and Mr. Vinegar took the gloves.

But the gloves were too small for Mr. Vinegar. As he tried to put them on he heard a parrot up in a tree calling to him: —

"Mr. Vinegar, Mr. Vinegar, gave his gold piece for a cow, gave his cow for a set of bagpipes, gave his bagpipes for a pair of little gloves. Ha, ha, ha."

That made Mr. Vinegar very cross. He threw his new gloves at the parrot, and they went so far up in the tree that he could not get them. Then Mr. Vinegar had nothing at all.

So Mr. Vinegar went home to Mrs. Vinegar, and he told her that he had been very foolish. And he found Mrs. Vinegar in a new house, busily sweeping as if nothing had happened. So it was all right, after all.

The Cat and the Mouse

ONCE UPON A TIME there was a cat who was playing with a mouse in a malt house. Now, whether the cat meant to do such a rude thing, or whether he did not, I do not know; but he bit off the mouse's tail.

And the poor little mouse said:—

"Please, Puss, give me back my tail again."

"No," said the puss, "I'll not give you back your tail unless you go to the cow and fetch me some milk."

Then off went the mouse, and—

First she leaped, and then she ran,
Till she came to the cow, and thus began:—

"Please, cow, give me some milk that I may give it to the cat, and she will give me back my little long tail."

"No," said the cow, "I will give you no milk until you go to the farmer and fetch me some hay."

Then off went the mouse, and—

First she leaped, and then she ran,
Till she came to the farmer, and thus began:—

"Please, farmer, give me some hay, that I may give it to the cow, and she will give me some milk for the cat, who will then give me back my little long tail."

"No," said the farmer, "I'll give you no hay until you fetch me some meat from the butcher."

Then off went the mouse, and—

First she leaped, and then she ran,
Till she came to the butcher, and thus began:—

"Please, butcher, give me some meat, that I may give it to the farmer, who will then give me hay for the cow, the cow will give me milk for the cat, and the cat will give me back my little long tail."

"No," said the butcher, "I will give you no meat until you fetch me some bread from the baker."

Then off went the mouse, and—

First she leaped, and then she ran,
Till she came to the baker, and thus began:—

"Please, baker, give me some bread for the butcher, then the butcher will give me meat for the farmer, the farmer will give me hay for the cow, the cow will give me milk for the cat, and the cat will give me back my little long tail."

"Well," said the baker, "I'll give you some bread,
But don't eat my meal, or I'll cut off your head."

So the good baker gave the mouse some bread; the mouse gave the bread to the butcher, who gave him some meat; the mouse gave the meat to the farmer, who gave him an armful of hay; the mouse gave the hay to the cow, and the cow gave the mouse a saucer of milk for the cat. Then the cat drank the milk, and gave the mouse his little long tail. And they went on playing in the malt house.

Chicken Little

ONCE UPON A TIME there was a tiny, tiny chicken, and her name was Chicken Little. One day Chicken Little was scratching in the garden where she should not have been, and a bit of a rose leaf fell upon her tail.

"Oh," cried Chicken Little, "the sky is falling. I must go tell the king."

So Chicken Little gaed and she gaed, and she met Henny Penny.

"Where do you travel so fast, Chicken Little?" asked Henny Penny.

"Ah, Henny Penny," said Chicken Little, "the sky is falling, and I must go and tell the king."

"How do you know that the sky is falling, Chicken Little?" asked Henny Penny.

"I saw it with my eyes, I heard it with my ears, and a bit of it fell upon my tail," said Chicken Little.

"I will go with you to the king," said Henny Penny.

17

So they ran along together, and they met Ducky Daddles.

"Where do you travel so fast?" asked Ducky Daddles.

"Ah, Ducky Daddles," said Chicken Little, "the sky is falling, and Henny Penny and I go to tell the king."

"How do you know that the sky is falling, Chicken Little?" asked Ducky Daddles.

"I saw it with my eyes, I heard it with my ears, and a bit of it fell upon my tail," said Chicken Little.

"I will go with you to the king," said Ducky Daddles.

So they ran along together, and they met Goosey Loosey.

"Where do you travel so fast, Chicken Little?" asked Goosey Loosey.

"Ah, Goosey Loosey," said Chicken Little, "the sky is falling. Henny Penny and Ducky Daddles and I go to tell the king."

"How do you know that the sky is falling, Chicken Little?" asked Goosey Loosey.

"I saw it with my eyes, I heard it with my ears, and a bit of it fell upon my tail," said Chicken Little.

"I will go with you," said Goosey Loosey.

So they ran along together, and they met Turkey Lurkey.

"Do you know the way to the king's house?" asked
Fox Lox.

"Where do you travel so fast, Chicken Little?" asked Turkey Lurkey.

"Ah, Turkey Lurkey," said Chicken Little, "the sky is falling, and Henny Penny and Ducky Daddles and Goosey Loosey and I go to tell the king."

"How do you know that the sky is falling?" asked Turkey Lurkey.

"I saw it with my eyes, I heard it with my ears, and a bit of it fell upon my tail," said Chicken Little.

"I will go with you to the king," said Turkey Lurkey.

So they ran along together, and they met Fox Lox.

"Where do you travel so fast, Chicken Little?" asked Fox Lox.

"Ah, Fox Lox," said Chicken Little, "the sky is falling, and we go to tell the king."

"Do you know the way to the king's house?" asked Fox Lox.

"No," said Chicken Little.

"No," said Henny Penny.

"No," said Ducky Daddles.

"No," said Goosey Loosey.

"No," said Turkey Lurkey.

"Then come with me and I will show you," said Fox Lox. And he led them all into his den, and they never, never came out again.

How Drakestail Went to the King

ONCE UPON A TIME there was a wee little duck with a very long tail, so he was called Drakestail. Now, Drakestail had some money of his very, very own, and the king asked if he might take it. So Drakestail loaned all his money to the king.

But the king kept Drakestail's money for a year and a day, and still he did not send it back. Drakestail said he would go to the king and fetch back the money himself.

So off he started, one very fine morning, for the king's house. The sun was shining on the ponds, and Drakestail waddled along in the middle of the road, feeling very fine. As he traveled, he met a fox, and the fox said, "Where do you go this fine morning, Friend Drakestail?"

"To the king," said Drakestail, "for he owes me money."

"I will travel along with you," said the fox.

"Ah," said Drakestail, "your four legs would

soon tire. Come along with me this way," and he opened his wee little bill very wide, and down his wee little throat went the fox.

Then Drakestail traveled on a little farther. As he went he came to a ladder lying beside the road.

"Where do you go this fine morning, Friend Drakestail?" asked the ladder.

"To the king," said Drakestail, "for he owes me money."

"I will travel along with you," said the ladder.

"Your wooden legs would soon tire," said Drakestail. "Come along with me this way," and he opened his little bill very wide, and down his wee little throat went the ladder.

Then Drakestail traveled on a bit farther until he came to his sweetheart, river, lying and glistening in the sunshine.

"Where do you go this fine morning, Friend Drakestail?" asked the river.

"To the king, for he owes me money," said Drakestail.

"I will travel with you," said the river.

"You would soon tire if you ran so far, sweetheart," said Drakestail. "Come along with me this way." He opened his wee bill very wide, and down his wee little throat went his sweetheart, little river.

Then Drakestail traveled and traveled until he came to the king's house. Now Drakestail thought that the king would meet him at the gate, so he called out very loudly:—

"*Honk! Honk!* Drakestail waits at the gate."

But the king did not come out to meet him. Who should appear at the gate but the king's cook, and the cook took Drakestail by his two little legs and flung him into the poultry yard. The other fowls, who were ill bred birds, ran up to Drakestail and bit him, and jeered at his large tail. It would have gone very badly with Drakestail, but he called to his friend, the fox:—

"Reynard, Reynard, come out to the earth,
    Or Drakestail's life is of little worth."

So the fox came out, and he ate up all the ill bred fowls in the king's poultry yard. But still Drakestail was badly off. He heard the king's cook putting the broth pot over the fire.

"Ladder, ladder, come out to the wall,
    Drakestail does not wish to be broth at all,"

he cried. So the ladder came out and leaned against the wall, and Drakestail climbed over in safety. But the king's cook saw Drakestail

and set out after him. He caught poor Drakestail and clapped him into the broth pot, and
hung him over the fire.

"River, my sweetheart, put out this hot fire,
The flames that would cook me rise higher
and higher,"

cried Drakestail. So the river put out the fire
with a great noise and sputtering, which the
king heard. And the king came running to the
kitchen.

"Good morning to you, king," said Drakestail, hopping out of the broth pot, and making
a very low bow, "are you through with my
money, which you have kept for a year and a
day?"

"That I am, Drakestail," said the king. "You
shall have it at once."

So the king gave Drakestail the money that
he owed him, and Drakestail waddled home
again to tell of all his travels.

Little Bear

ONCE UPON A TIME, there was an Indian boy and he had a little sister. Now the little sister was not like a common child, for she was a bear.

Early one morning, the boy started out to seek his fortune, but Little Bear wished to go too.

"No, no, Little Bear, you cannot go. You must stay at home and watch the fire," said her brother. Then he tied Little Bear to the door posts that she might not run away.

He had not gone very far on his journey when he heard, TRAMP, TRAMP, TRAMP, in the path behind him. There was Little Bear following with the door posts on her back.

"Oh, Little Bear, I told you to stay at home and watch the fire," said the boy.

He led Little Bear back, and this time he tied her to a pine tree.

He had not gone very far when he heard once more, TRAMP, TRAMP, TRAMP, in the

path behind him. There was Little Bear following with the pine tree on her back.

"Oh, Little Bear, you must stay at home and
watch the fire," said the boy.

He led Little Bear back, and this time he
tied her to a rock.

He started on his journey again, but he had
not gone a stone's throw, when he heard,
THUMP, THUMP, THUMP, in the path behind
him. There was Little Bear following him with
the rock on her back.

"What shall I do with you, Little Bear?" said
the boy. But just then they came to a wide
brook with no bridge to span it.

"How shall I cross?" said the little boy.

Little Bear pushed the rock into the water.
She laid the pine tree across the rock for a
bridge. They both walked across the brook in
safety.

"Well, you may come with me, Little Bear,"
said the boy.

They journeyed for many days until they
came, at last, to some very dark woods. In the
woods they met Brother Wolf carrying a candle to light him on his way.

"The sun is lost from the sky," said Brother
Wolf; "the old squaw pulled it down."

"Oho, I can find the sun," said Little Bear,
"but you must first give me two lumps of
maple sugar."

Brother Wolf gave Little Bear two lumps of maple sugar and she hurried along until she came to the old squaw's wigwam. The old squaw was stirring a kettle of rice over her fire. Little Bear crept up behind her. Little Bear dropped the two lumps of maple sugar into the kettle. As the old squaw stirred, she tasted her rice.

"It is too sweet," she said; "I must go to the fields for more."

While she was gone, Little Bear found the sun which the old squaw had hid in her wigwam. Little Bear tossed it back to the sky again.

When the old squaw came back from the rice fields and missed her sun, she was very angry. She looked for it many, many days, but the clouds hid it from her. Then, one night, she pulled the moon down, and hid that away in her wigwam.

So there was no light in the evening. Brother Wolf lighted his candle again, and he hurried after the boy and Little Bear, who had started on their journey again.

"The moon is gone from the sky," said Brother Wolf, "the old squaw has pulled it down."

"Oho, I can find the moon," said Little Bear; "give me two pinches of salt, Brother Wolf."

Brother Wolf gave Little Bear two pinches

of salt, and Little Bear crept up to the old squaw again, and threw the salt in her kettle of rice.

"The rice is too salt," said the old squaw, tasting as she stirred; "I must go to the field for more."

While she was gone, Little Bear snatched the moon from the wigwam, where the old squaw had hid it, and tossed it up to the sky again.

Brother Wolf snuffed his candle, for he did not need it any more, but the old squaw was very angry. The old squaw ran after Little Bear. She caught her, and she put her in a bag, and tied the bag to a tree. Then she went for her spoon with which to beat Little Bear.

But while she was gone, Little Bear bit a hole in the bag with her teeth. She slipped out. Then she filled the bag with the old squaw's pots and pans. When the old squaw came back, and began beating the bag, she broke all her dishes.

Then the boy and Little Bear picked up enough sun gold and moon silver which had fallen by the road to make them rich for always. And Little Bear traveled with her brother wherever he went after that. Was she not a clever Little Bear?

The Story of Lambikin

ONCE UPON A TIME there was a wee, wee Lambikin, and he thought he would go over the hill to see his granny.

So he frolicked along on his teetery legs, as happy and frisky as ever a Lambikin in the spring could be.

But he had not gone very far when he met a roaring lion, and the lion said:—

"Lambikin, I will eat you."

Then Lambikin could not think what to do, for he did not wish to be eaten just then. So he said to the lion:—

> "Lambikin goes to Grannikin,
>   Where fatter he will grow,
>   Then you may eat him so."

The lion wanted a very fat lamb to eat, so he let Lambikin go on his way, but he said:—

"Be sure to come back this way, Lambikin."

Well, Lambikin frolicked along on his teetery legs a little farther, when he suddenly saw a great vulture, with a huge bill, flying toward him.

"I will eat you, Lambikin," said the vulture.

Now Lambikin was not ready to be eaten yet, so he said to the vulture:—

> "Lambikin goes to Grannikin,
>   Where fatter he will grow,
>   Then you may eat him so."

And the vulture flew off, but he said to Lambikin as he went:—

"Be sure to come back this way, Lambikin."

Well, Lambikin frolicked along a little farther on his teetery legs, when he suddenly saw a striped tiger coming to meet him, and the tiger said to him:—

"Lambikin, I will eat you."

Now Lambikin did not wish to be eaten by a striped tiger, so he said:—

> "Lambikin goes to Grannikin,
>   Where fatter he will grow,
>   Then you may eat him so."

The tiger was sure that a fat lamb would taste better than a wee, wee one with teetery legs, so he let Lambikin go along, but he said as he went:—

Lambikin frolicked along a little farther on his teetery legs, when he suddenly saw a striped tiger.

"Be sure that you come back this way, Lambikin."

Well, Lambikin reached his granny's house, and he told her how glad he was to see her, and then he said he was very hungry, and he would like something to eat.

"I must grow fat, granny," said Lambikin.

So his granny led the way to the corn bin, and Lambikin ate and ate and ate until his sides stuck out, and his legs were not teetery any more, and he was a fat little lamb. But the more corn he ate and the fatter he grew the less did he want to be eaten. So he said to his granny: —

"Grannikin, lion and vulture and tiger will eat Lambikin. What shall he do?"

Then said his granny: —

"I will make a drum of a bit of old skin. Do you get inside and roll past the lion and the vulture and the tiger."

So granny made a drum of a bit of skin, and Lambikin jumped inside the drum, and off he rolled toward home.

But before he had gone very far he met the lion, who was waiting for him, and the lion said: —

"Drummikin, have you seen Lambikin?"

But Lambikin called out from inside the drum: —

"Fallen into the fire, and so will you.
    On, little Drummikin, tum, tum, too."

Then the lion thought the woods must be on fire, so he ran off as fast as he could.

But Lambikin had not gone very far when the vulture flew down for his dinner.

"Drummikin, have you seen Lambikin?" asked the vulture.

"Fallen into the fire, and so will you.
    On, little Drummikin, tum, tum, too,"

said Lambikin in a gruff voice from the inside of the drum.

Then the vulture thought that the woods must surely be on fire, so he flew far above the treetops.

Lambikin rolled merrily along a little way farther, but soon he met the striped tiger, who was waiting for his dinner.

"Drummikin, have you seen Lambikin?" asked the striped tiger.

"Fallen in the fire, and so will you.
    On, little Drummikin, tum, tum, too,"

said Lambikin; but the striped tiger had very sharp ears.

"Lambikin is inside Drummikin," he said,

and he started after the drum as fast as he could go. He nearly caught it, for he went so very fast, but they came to a bramble bush. The tiger caught his tail and was not able to move, and out of the drum jumped Lambikin.

Then off he frolicked home again as frisky and happy as ever a lamb could be.

Johnny Cake

ONCE UPON A TIME, when it was long ago, there lived an old man and an old woman and a little boy.

One day the old woman was making bread, and she stirred up a johnny cake and put it in the oven to bake. Then she went off to the fields to work with the old man, and the little boy was left to watch the oven. Well, the little boy did watch the oven for a little while, and then he grew very sleepy. His head nid, nodded, and soon he was asleep on the kitchen floor.

Now this was just what the johnny cake wanted. He opened the oven door a crack, and down he hopped to the hearth, and out through the kitchen door he ran.

"Hip, hip, hurrah!" called Johnny Cake, as he ran along. "Here I go off by myself to see the world."

But as he ran he passed the field where the little old man and the little old woman were working, and they saw him. Down they dropped their rakes and after Johnny Cake they ran as fast as ever they could go, but they were not quick enough for him.

Johnny Cake skipped along the road, and after a while he came to two ditch diggers. The ditch diggers dropped their shovels, and they ran after Johnny Cake, too, but they were not quick enough for him. Johnny Cake called out to them as he skipped along:—

"I have outrun an old woman, and an old man, and a little boy. I can outrun you-ooo."

So Johnny Cake skipped along the road, and after a while he came to a bear sitting beside a tree. The bear got up, and started after Johnny Cake, but he was not quick enough for him. Johnny Cake called back to him:—

"I have outrun an old woman, and an old man, and a little boy, and two ditch diggers. I can outrun you-ooo."

Then Johnny Cake skipped on down the road, and by and by he came to a fox. "Where are you going, Johnny Cake?" asked the fox.

"Oh," said Johnny Cake, "I have outrun an old man, and an old woman, and a little boy, and two ditch diggers, and a bear. I can outrun you-ooo."

"What did you say, Johnny Cake?" asked the

fox, putting his paw to his ear. "I am a little hard of hearing."

"*I have outrun an old woman, and an old man, and a little boy, and two ditch diggers, and a bear,*" said Johnny Cake, "*I can outrun you-ooo,*" and he stepped a little closer so that the fox could hear him.

"What is that you are saying?" said the fox. "I am very hard of hearing, you know. Step up closer, please." So Johnny Cake went up close to the fox's ear, and shouted very loudly:—

"I HAVE OUTRUN AN OLD WOMAN, AND AN OLD MAN, AND A LITTLE BOY, AND TWO DITCH DIGGERS, AND A BEAR. I CAN OUT-RUN YOU-OOO."

"I don't think you can, Johnny Cake," said the fox, as he opened his mouth wide, and ate him up.

The Wonderful Pot

ONCE UPON A TIME there lived a little boy and his mother, and they were very, very poor because a rich man had stolen all their money. They lived in a tiny hut, and all they owned in the world was a cow.

At last, one day, they had not a bite left to eat.

"You must sell the cow," the mother said to the little boy. So the little boy took the cow's halter and started down the road to sell her.

On the way he met a stranger, and the stranger took from under his cloak a little black iron pot with three legs.

"Will you give me your cow if I give you this wonderful pot?" asked the stranger.

"Not I," said the little boy; but just then he heard a wee voice. It was the little iron pot talking.

"Take me, do," said the pot. So the little boy gave the cow to the stranger. He took the pot

home and he put it in the barn in the cow's stall.

"Ah, me, what a bad bargain you have made, son," said the mother when she saw no money, only a three-legged pot in the barn. But the pot began dancing about in the cow's stall.

"Clean me, and put me over the fire," said the wonderful pot. So the mother washed the pot and set it over the fire, but, ah, she had naught with which to fill it.

"I skip, I skip," said the pot, jumping down from the fire and running across the floor.

"How far do you skip?" asked the mother.

"To the rich man's house," said the pot, skipping out of the door and up the road as fast as its three legs would carry it.

Now the rich man's wife was making a pudding.

"Ah," she cried, when she saw the pot skip up to her door, "you are just what I needed to boil my pudding in."

She filled the pot with good things, flour and butter and sugar and fruit and spices.

"Now boil," she said, setting the pudding over the fire. So the pudding boiled and boiled and boiled, but when it was done, tap, tap, went the three little legs. The pot jumped

from the fire and skipped out of the door and down the road.

"Where are you going with my pudding?" called the rich man's wife, running after the pot.

"Home again," called the pot, and the rich man's wife could not stop it. So the poor little boy and his mother had all the pudding they could eat.

Next morning the wonderful pot said again, "I skip, I skip."

"How far do you skip?" asked the mother.

"To the rich man's barn," said the pot, skipping down the road as fast as its three little legs could take it. It stopped at the barn door. Inside, the threshers were threshing grain.

"See the fine little pot," cried the threshers; "how much wheat will it hold?"

Then the threshers poured a peck of wheat into the pot, but there was room for more. They poured in a bushel of wheat. There was still room for more. They poured and poured until the pot held all of the rich man's wheat.

Tap, tap, went the three little legs, and out of the door skipped the pot, and down the road.

"Where are you going?" called the threshers, running after it.

"Home again," called back the wonderful pot, and the threshers could not catch it.

So the poor little boy and his mother had all the wheat bread that they could eat.

Next morning, the wonderful pot said again: —

"I skip, I skip."

"How far do you skip?" asked the mother.

"To the rich man's counting house," said the pot, skipping down the road as fast as its three legs could take it.

It was a beautiful day, and the rich man sat in his counting house spreading his gold out in the sunlight to keep it from growing mouldy.

The wonderful pot skipped up to the window, and jumped up on the table.

"Just what I need to measure my gold," said the rich man, and he filled the pot full to the rim with gold dollars.

Tap, tap, went the three little legs. Out of the window jumped the pot, and down the road it hastened.

"Where are you going?" called the rich man.

"Home again," called back the pot, and the rich man could not catch it. So the poor little boy and his mother had all the gold which the rich man had stolen from them.

The fourth day the wonderful pot said as before:—

"I skip, I skip."

"Why do you skip, little pot?" asked the mother, for they needed nothing, having pudding, and bread, and gold.

"To fetch the rich man," said the little pot, and off it skipped. But as soon as the rich man spied it skipping gayly along the road on its three little legs, he cried:—

"Ah, you wicked little pot. You took my pudding, and my wheat, and my gold. I will break you to bits."

So he laid hold of the little pot's handle, but there he stuck, and he could not let go no matter how he pulled. He became smaller, and smaller, until he found himself inside the pot.

"I skip, I skip," said the wonderful pot for the last time. Tap, tap, went the three little legs, and the pot skipped gayly off with the rich man inside, and nobody knew where they went, for they never came back again.

The Three Bears

ONCE UPON A TIME there were three bears who lived in a house of their own in the woods. There was a small, wee bear, there was a middle-sized bear, and there was a great, huge bear. They had each a pot for their porridge. There was a little pot for the small, wee bear, and a middle-sized pot for the middle-sized bear, and a great pot for the great, huge bear.

And they had each a chair to sit in. There was a little chair for the small, wee bear, and a middle-sized chair for the middle-sized bear, and a great chair for the great, huge bear.

And they had each a bed to sleep in at night. There was a little bed for the small, wee bear, there was a middle-sized bed for the middle-sized bear, and there was a great bed for the great, huge bear.

One morning the three bears left their porridge cooling in their porridge pots, and they went for a walk in the woods that they might not burn their mouths by eating it too soon; and while they were out walking, along came a little old woman to their house.

First, she peeped in the window; and then she peeped in the keyhole, and then she opened the door and went inside.

She was well pleased to see the three bowls of porridge cooling on the table. First she tasted the porridge of the great, huge bear, but that was too hot. Then she tasted the porridge of the middle-sized bear, but that was too cold. Then she tasted the porridge of the small, wee bear, and that was neither too hot nor too cold, but just right, and the little old woman ate and she ate until it was all gone.

Then the little old woman went poking about the house to see what she could find, and she came, all at once, upon the three chairs. So, first, she sat down in the chair of the great, huge bear, but that was too high for her. Then she sat down in the chair of the middle-sized bear, but that was too hard for her. And last of all, she sat down in the chair of the small, wee bear, which was neither too hard nor too high, but just right, and there she sat until she sat the bottom right out, and fell, plump, upon the floor.

Then the little old woman went up the stairs, and she came to the bears' bedroom. First she tried the bed of the great, huge bear, but that was too high for her. Then she lay down in the bed of the middle-sized bear, but that was too hard for her. And, last of all, she lay down in the bed of the small, wee bear, and that was neither too high nor too hard, but just right; and there she lay until she went fast asleep.

After a while the three bears came home, and they knew at once that some one had been at their porridge.

"WHO HAS BEEN EATING MY PORRIDGE?" asked the great, huge bear, in his great, huge voice.

"Who has been eating my porridge?" asked the middle-sized bear, in his middle-sized voice.

"Dear me," said the small, wee bear, in his small, wee voice, "some one has been eating my porridge, and here it is all gone."

And then the three bears spied their three chairs.

"WHO HAS BEEN SITTING IN MY CHAIR?" asked the great, huge bear, in his great, huge voice.

"Who has been sitting in my chair?" asked the middle-sized bear, in his middle-sized voice.

And you know what the little old woman had done to the chair of the small, wee bear.

"Some one has been sitting in my chair and

has sat the bottom right out of it," said the small, wee bear, in his small, wee voice.

So the three bears thought they would better go up to their bedroom, and they soon saw that some one had been there, too.

"WHO HAS BEEN LYING IN MY BED?" said the great, huge bear, in his great, huge voice.

"Who has been lying in my bed?" asked the middle-sized bear, in his middle-sized voice.

And when the small, wee bear came to look at his bed, you know who was there.

"Some one has been lying in my bed, and here she is," said the small, wee bear, in his small, wee voice.

Then the little old woman awoke, and when she saw the three bears looking down on her from one side of the bed, she was very much afraid, and she jumped out at the other. Over to the window she ran, and down to the ground she jumped, and home she went as fast as her feet would take her. And after that she never went into the houses of other people where she had not been asked.

"Some one has been lying in my bed, and here she is."

The Little Boy Who Found His Fortune

ONCE UPON A TIME there were two little brothers, and the first set out to seek his father's lost fortune. He went a long, long way through the world. When it was nearly night he came to a wee, red house in the midst of a wood. In the doorway stood an old witch.

"May I sleep in your house all night, Goody?" asked the little boy.

"You may," said the witch.

So the little boy went into the house, and slept all night.

Early in the morning, the little boy awoke. The old witch sat by her table snoring. On the table lay his father's bag of gold.

The little boy seized the bag of gold, and ran out of the house as fast as ever he could. He ran, and ran until he came to a Meeting House.

"Little boy, little boy, come in and sweep me," said the Meeting House.

"Not I," said the little boy, and he ran the faster.

48

Soon he came to a Field.

"Little boy, little boy, come and weed me," said the Field.

"Not I," said the little boy, and he ran the faster.

Soon he came to a Well.

"Little boy, little boy, come and clean me," said the Well.

"Not I," said the little boy, and he ran, and ran until he came to a tree. And he sat down beneath the tree to count the gold.

But the old witch awoke, and she missed the gold. She ran after the little boy, and presently she came to the Meeting House.

"Have you seen a boy,
With a wig and a wag,
And a long leather bag?" said she.

"Yes," said the Meeting House, "a little boy passed by this way."

The old witch ran on and on, and she came to the Field.

"Have you seen a little boy,
With a wig and a wag,
And a long leather bag?" said she.

"Yes," said the Field, "a little boy passed by this way."

The old woman ran on and on, and she came to the Well.

"Have you seen a little boy,
  With a wig and a wag,
  And a long leather bag?" said she.

"Yes," said the Well, "the little boy sits under a tree." So the old witch came to the tree. She took the bag of gold away from the little boy, and he was obliged to go home without his fortune.

The next day the second little brother set out to seek his father's gold. He, too, went a long, long way, and he came to the wee, red house in the wood where the old witch lived.

"May I sleep here for the night, Goody?" asked the second little boy.

"You may," said the old witch.

So the second little brother went into the house, and slept all night.

Early in the morning he awoke. There sat the old witch, snoring, and her bag of gold lay on the table. The second little boy seized the bag, and ran out of the door.

He ran, and he ran until he came to the Meeting House.

"Little boy, little boy, sweep me," said the Meeting House.

"That I will gladly," said the little boy.

It was a very large Meeting House, but he set down his bag of gold, and swept it clean.

Then he ran on again, but soon he came to the Field.

"Little boy, little boy, weed me," said the Field.

It was a very large Field, but the little boy set down his bag of gold, and weeded it from corner to corner.

Then he ran and ran until he came to the Well.

"Little boy, little boy, clean me," said the Well.

"That I will," said the little boy, and though it was a very deep Well, he set down his bag of gold and cleaned it from top to bottom.

Then he ran until he came to a tree, and he sat down beneath it to count his fortune.

But the old witch soon missed her gold, and she followed after the second little boy. She came to the Meeting House.

> "Have you seen a boy,
>   With a wig and a wag,
>   And a long leather bag?" said she.

The Meeting House said never a word, but threw stones at the old witch.

So the old witch hastened to the Field.

> "Have you seen a boy,
> With a wig and a wag,
> And a long leather bag?" said she.

The Field said not a word, but it blew a cloud of dust in the old witch's eyes.

Then she hurried on until she came to the Well.

> "Have you seen a boy,
> With a wig and a wag,
> And a long leather bag?" said she.

The Well said never a word, but threw a bucket of water in her face, so the old witch went home again.

And the second little boy took his bag of gold and went home, too, for he had found his fortune.

The Little Old Woman Who Went to the North Wind

ONCE UPON A TIME there was a little old woman who wished to make for herself a loaf of wheat bread. So she hastened to the miller and bought a pan of white flour. As she opened her gate, and came into her garden, HUFF, PUFF, along came the North Wind, and he blew her flour far and wide to the four corners of the world.

So the little old woman hastened again to the miller, and she bought a second pan of flour. But no sooner had she reached her garden again, than, HUFF, PUFF, along came the North Wind, and he blew the second pan of flour to the four corners of the world.

Then the little old woman went a third time to the miller and bought flour, but a third time did the North Wind blow away the flour.

"I will go to the North Wind," said the little old woman, "and ask him to give me back my three panfuls of flour."

So the little old woman went a long, long way until she came to the North Wind sitting astride a huge mountain top.

"How do you do?" asked the little old woman, politely.

"Thanks to yourself," said the North Wind in a thick voice, "and what would you like to-day?"

"Three pans of flour which you took from me," said the little old woman.

"Now, those three pans of flour I could never give you," said the North Wind, "for I blew them far and wide to the four corners of the world; but I will give you my magic tablecloth. Whenever you say to it, 'Cloth, spread yourself,' it will be at once covered with fine eating and drinking."

So the little old woman thanked the North Wind, and took the magic tablecloth, and started home. But the way was so long that she stopped at an inn for the night. Before she went to bed, she thought she would like something to eat, so she spread the magic tablecloth upon the floor, and she said to it:—

"Cloth, spread yourself."

In a second the cloth was covered with such fine eating and drinking as the little old woman had never seen before. There were puddings, and jam, and tarts, and cakes, and ice cream, and lemonade. The little old woman sat down and ate her fill, but as she was eating, the innkeeper, who had smelled the feast, peeped through the keyhole.

"A very fine tablecloth for me," thought the innkeeper.

So, when the little old woman was sleeping, the innkeeper took the North Wind's magic tablecloth, and hid it in his cupboard.

When the little old woman awoke in the morning, she looked, and looked, and looked for her tablecloth, but she could not find it. Then she hurried back to the North Wind and told him what had happened.

"Well," said the North Wind, "I must give you my magic staff. Say to it, 'Staff, dance,' and the person whose toes it dances upon, that person has the magic tablecloth."

So the little old woman thanked the North Wind, and she hurried back to the inn with the magic staff.

There sat the innkeeper and all his guests with the magic tablecloth spread between them. They were eating and drinking good things.

"Staff, dance," said the little old woman, loudly.

Then the magic staff began to dance right merrily, up and down, to and fro, right and

left. But wherever the innkeeper went, the
staff followed, treading upon his toes, until he
called out:—

"Enough, enough, here is your magic tablecloth."

Then the magic staff danced away to the
North Wind again, and the little old woman
took her tablecloth home.

And she never had want of anything after
that, for the magic tablecloth was always
ready to spread itself for her with fine eating
and drinking.

Brother Rabbit.

Why the Bear Sleeps All Winter

ONCE UPON A TIME, little Brother Rabbit
lived, quite sober and industrious, in the
woods, and just close by lived a big, brown
Bear.

Now little Brother Rabbit never troubled
his neighbors in those days, nor meddled with
their housekeeping, nor played any tricks the
way he does now. In the fall, he gathered his
acorns, and his pig nuts, and his rabbit
tobacco. On a frosty morning, he would set
out with Brother Fox for the farmer's; and
while Brother Fox looked after the chicken
yards, little Brother Rabbit picked cabbage,
and pulled turnips, and gathered carrots and
parsnips for his cellar. When the winter came,
he never failed to share his store with a wan-
dering field mouse, or a traveling chipmunk.

Now, in those days, old Bear was not con-
tent to do his own housekeeping, and doze in
the sun, and gather wild honey in the summer,
and fish through the ice in the winter. He was

full of mischief, and was always playing tricks. Of all the beasts of the wood, the one he loved best to trouble was sober little Brother Rabbit.

Just as soon as Brother Rabbit moved to a new tree stump, and filled his bins with vegetables, and his pantry with salad, along came old Bear and carried off all his stores.

Just as soon as Brother Rabbit filled his house with dry, warm leaves for a bed, creepy, creepy, crawly, along came old Bear, and tried to squeeze himself into the bed, too, and of course he was too big.

At last, Brother Rabbit could stand it no longer, and he went to all the beasts in the wood to ask their advice.

The first one he met was Brother Frog, sitting on the edge of the pond, and sticking his feet in the nice, cool mud.

"What shall I do, Brother Frog?" asked Brother Rabbit; "Brother Bear will not leave me alone."

"Let us ask Brother Squirrel," said Brother Frog.

So the two went to Brother Squirrel, cracking nuts in the hickory tree.

"What shall we do, Brother Squirrel?" asked Brother Frog; "Brother Bear will not leave Brother Rabbit alone."

"Let us ask Brother Mole," said Brother Squirrel, dropping his nuts.

So the three went to where Brother Mole was digging the cellar for a new house, and they said:—

"What shall we do, Brother Mole? Brother Bear will not leave Brother Rabbit alone."

"Let us ask Brother Fox," said Brother Mole.

So Brother Mole, and Brother Squirrel, and Brother Frog, and Brother Rabbit went to where Brother Fox was combing his brush behind a bush, and they said to him:—

"What shall we do, Brother Fox? Brother Bear will not leave Brother Rabbit alone."

"Let us go to Brother Bear," said Brother Fox.

So they all went along with little Brother Rabbit, and they hunted and hunted for old Bear, but they could not find him. They hunted and hunted some more, and they peeped in a hollow tree. There lay old Bear, fast asleep.

"Hush," said Brother Fox.

Then he whispered to Brother Frog, "Bring a little mud."

And he whispered to Brother Squirrel, "Bring some leaves."

And he whispered to Brother Mole, "Bring some dirt, little brother."

And to Brother Rabbit he said, "Stand ready to do what I tell you."

So Brother Frog brought mud, Brother Squirrel brought leaves, Brother Mole brought dirt, and Brother Rabbit stood ready.

Then Brother Fox said to Brother Rabbit, "Stop up the ends of Brother Bear's log."

So Brother Rabbit took the mud and the leaves and the dirt, and he stopped up the ends of the log. Then he hammered hard with his two back feet, which are good for hammering. And they all went home, for they thought that old Bear would never, never get out of the log.

Well, old Bear slept and slept, but after a while he awoke, and he opened one eye. He saw no sunshine, so he thought it was still night, and he went to sleep again.

After another while, he awoke again, but he heard the rain and sleet beating outside, and it was very warm and dry inside.

"What a very long night," said old Bear, and he curled up his paws, and he went to sleep again.

This time, he just slept, and slept, until it began to be very warm inside the log, and he heard in his dreams the footsteps of birds outside.

Then he awoke, and he stretched himself,

and he shook himself. He rubbed his eyes with his paws, and he poked away the mud, and the leaves, and the dirt, and he went outside.

But was he not surprised?

It had been a frosty night when he had gone to sleep, and now the woods were green. Old Bear had slept all winter.

"That was a fine, long sleep," said old Bear, as he set out for little Brother Rabbit's house to see if he had anything good for breakfast; "I shall sleep again, next fall."

So every summer, old Bear plays tricks on little Brother Rabbit, but when the fall comes, he creeps away to a warm, dark place to sleep until spring.

And so have his grandchildren, and his great-grandchildren ever since.

Little Footsteps Upon the Water

ONCE UPON A TIME there was a little Indian boy, and his name was Footsteps Upon the Water, because he could run so fast and so still.

One day, little Footsteps Upon the Water was chasing a squirrel, and he ran so far and so wide that he went far from home, and he could not find his way back. On and on ran the squirrel until it came at last to a hollow log, and it went inside to hide. Footsteps Upon the Water went inside, too, but he was not so small as the squirrel. Out of the log ran the squirrel, but the little boy could not get out. He was stuck fast inside the hollow log.

His father looked for the little boy many moons. His mother sat at home in the wig-wam, crying, but Footsteps Upon the Water did not come back. He lay in the log, and he pounded and shouted, and he thought no one was ever coming to let him out.

But one morning, as he rapped, he heard, on

the outside, *rap*, *rap*, *rap*, and a shrill voice calling:—

"Footsteps Upon the Water, are you there? Are you there?"

Then a wrinkled, brown face, with a fringe of arrows for a cap, peered in at the end of the log. It was Grandmother Porcupine come to help the little boy out.

"I traveled three days, and three nights, little Footsteps Upon the Water, because I heard you cry," said Grandmother Porcupine.

Then she scratched and she scratched at the end of the log, but she could not get the little boy out.

"I will fetch my three grandsons," said Grandmother Porcupine, and she hurried away to the old hemlock tree where her grandsons lived. She brought them back with her, and they all scratched at the end of the hollow log until at last the little boy was able to crawl out.

Footsteps Upon the Water winked and blinked his eyes when he came outside, for he had not seen the sun in many days. There, in a circle, sat Grandmother Porcupine, her three grandsons, the old Bear, the Deer, and the Wolf.

"Now, who will be a mother to this little boy?" said Grandmother Porcupine; "I am too old to take care of him."

There, in a circle, sat Grandmother Porcupine, her three grandsons, the old Bear, the Deer, and the Wolf.

"I will be his mother," said the Wolf.

"No, indeed," said Grandmother Porcupine, "your teeth are too sharp."

"I will be his mother," said the Deer.

"No, indeed," said Grandmother Porcupine, "you are always traveling. Your husband would carry little Footsteps Upon the Water on his back wherever he went, and the little boy would have no home in the winter."

"I will be his mother," said the good old Bear; "I have a warm house in the rocks with plenty to eat in my pantry,—berries, and nuts, and honey."

"You may have little Footsteps Upon the Water," said Grandmother Porcupine, "but be sure that your cubs do not teach him any rough tricks."

So Footsteps Upon the Water went home to the Bear's house, a cave in the rocks, with little rooms just like a real house. It was a fine place to live.

All summer the little boy played with the cubs. When it was late in the fall, and the days were short and dark, and the nights were cold, Mother Bear tucked them all in bed and they slept until spring.

Then came another summer, and other Bear people stopped to call upon them, saying:—

"We know a fine berry patch."

So they would all go away together to pick strawberries, or blackberries, or gooseberries. After a while, they went for chestnuts, and that was the most fun of all.

But Mother Bear taught Footsteps Upon the Water and the little cubs to run always, when they saw a man with a bow and arrows. One day, a man came very close to the Bear's house, but Mother Bear chased him with a forked stick, and he went away.

The next day, the man came again, just as the family was starting out for chestnuts. Mother Bear threw a bag of feathers at the man so that he was not able to see, and he ran away.

The third day, the man came again. Mother Bear was starting out for a neighbor's house with a bundle upon her back. She chased the man with her forked stick, she threw some more feathers at him, but it did no good. The man shot an arrow at Mother Bear, and she fell to the ground.

"Oh, good Mother Bear," cried little Footsteps Upon the Water, running out to help her, "such a cruel man to hurt my good Mother Bear."

But the arrow had stuck fast in Mother

Bear's bundle, and she was not hurt at all. And the man ran up to little Footsteps Upon the Water, crying:—

"My little lost boy, my little lost boy," for it was Footsteps Upon the Water's own father.

Then he told Mother Bear how sorry he was that he had tried to hurt her, and he invited her and all the cubs to come for a visit to the wigwam.

And little Footsteps Upon the Water went home, but he never forgot how good old Mother Bear had been to him.

The Gold Bugs

ONCE UPON A TIME there were two
green and glittering gold bugs, and one
said to the other: —

"The day is warm and sunny, let us go out
and play."

"We will," said the second gold bug, and
they decided to play at dancing.

So the two green, glittering gold bugs went
down to a brook near by, and there, shining and floating above the water, they saw
two glorious dragon flies, one green, and one
blue.

"We will dance with these dragon flies," said
one gold bug. "I choose the blue one."

"You cannot have her," said the other gold
bug, "I choose her."

"I will dance with the blue dragon fly," said
the first gold bug.

"You shall not dance with the blue dragon
fly," said the second gold bug.

So they quarreled until two other gold bugs

came along, and asked the dragon flies to dance with them, so that was an end of the matter.

The two green and glittering gold bugs then said they would play at something else.

"We will play hide and seek," said the first gold bug.

"No, we will play tag," said the second gold bug.

"I will play nothing but hide and seek," said the first gold bug.

"And I will play nothing but tag," said the second gold bug.

"I am going to hide," said the first gold bug; so he went away and hid himself beneath a clover leaf, but, ah, there was no one to go and look for him.

"I will run," said the second gold bug; so he ran, but, ah, there was no one to catch him. It was not fun to play that way, and there was an end of the matter.

The two green and glittering gold bugs then said they would play at something else, so they went to a tall bell flower to swing.

"I will sit inside, and you shall rock me," said the first gold bug.

"No, I will sit inside first, and you shall rock me," said the second gold bug.

So they quarreled as to which should swing

first, and in their quarreling they tore a petal of the beautiful bell flower, so they could not swing at all, and there was an end of the matter.

"Tut, tut, what is the meaning of this?" asked an old gold bug who came crawling along just then. "Why do you two green and glittering young things quarrel this bright morning?"

"We cannot play, and we are very unhappy, grandfather," said the two gold bugs. "We do not wish to play the same games."

"Silly, silly," said the old gold bug, and as he crawled away, he turned his head about, and he said, "Take turns, take turns. Turn about is fair play."

Now it had never occurred to the two green and glittering gold bugs that to take turns is the best way to play, and they decided to try.

They went back to the brook, and there were the two beautiful dragon flies, again floating over the water. So the first gold bug danced with the green dragon fly, and the second gold bug danced with the blue dragon fly; and then they changed about until they could dance no longer.

After that they played tag, and the first gold bug chased the second gold bug until they were tired. Then the first gold bug hid himself,

and the second gold bug tried to find him, which was very good fun indeed.

And last of all they found another bell flower, and they rocked each other all the afternoon, until it was time to go home.

So they had a very good day after all, did those green and glittering gold bugs, for they had learned that to take turns is the best way to play.

The Discontented Coffee Pot

ONCE UPON A TIME there was an old cook, who lived in a very fine kitchen. There were chives growing in the window, and pots and kettles of all sorts and sizes hanging upon the wall. There was a shining copper kettle on the stove, and upon the shelf stood the big black coffee pot, and the fat blue cream pitcher. One day, the old cook washed the windows, and swept and scoured the floor, and then sifted fine white sand in beautiful trailing patterns all over it. She polished her stove until she could see her own face in it. Then she sat down by the fire with a pan of rosy apples in her lap and began paring them. On the floor the apple parings fell, and they coiled and coiled about the old cook's feet, and they piled up higher and higher. The tea kettle bubbled on the stove and the old cook's head began to nod. The apple parings piled higher and higher until they came up to

her lap, she thought, and she nidded and nodded, and at last the old cook was fast asleep.

Then there was, all at once, a rattling of handles among the pots and kettles upon the wall. The tea kettle took off his cover politely to the green chives upon the window sill, and on the shelf the black coffee pot tripped over to the fat blue cream pitcher and leaned against its handle in a friendly manner, as he sighed through his spout and said sadly:—

"Nothing but coffee, nothing but coffee the whole year long."

"Nothing but milk, nothing but milk," sighed the fat blue cream pitcher in reply.

"Look at the blue bowl," said the discontented coffee pot, "cake dough, and crullers, and pretzels."

"And the platter," said the fat blue cream pitcher, "venison and sausages."

"I think I will fetch me a bit of venison to hold," said the discontented coffee pot.

"What a wonderful creature you are," said the fat blue cream pitcher; "could you buy me a bit of sausage to hold at the same time?"

"I will certainly try," said the coffee pot, as he leaned carefully over the edge of the shelf, and started to jump to the floor.

But the tea kettle had heard them, and he sputtered and bubbled his disapproval.

"Don't do it, don't do it," he said. "It's against the order of the kitchen. No coffee pot and cream pitcher ever did such a thing before."

"Well," said the fat cream pitcher, "perhaps you are right after all. Milk I have held, and milk I must hold until I crack. Never mind the sausage, friend coffee pot."

But the coffee pot was not like minded. He toppled off the shelf and went rattling across the floor to the pantry as if he did not hear the tea kettle still groaning, "It's against the order of things, the order of the kitchen, and no good will come of it."

Now the venison was all gone from the pantry. The coffee pot looked about, under shelves and on top of shelves. He poked his nose in the sugar barrel, and at last he saw on the blue platter a fine long link of sausages.

"Now I shall hold sausage," said the discontented coffee pot. "At last I shall have something different."

So he opened his cover, and he swallowed the sausages, and rattled back across the kitchen and climbed to his shelf again.

Then there arose such a clatter in the kitchen because of the unusual thing that the coffee pot had done. The cream pitcher and the tea kettle told every one, and there began such a rattling of lids and covers, and dancing of china plates that it seemed as if all the dishes would be broken, and because of all the noise, the old cook awoke.

"It is nearly tea time," she said. "What a din the wind in the chimney makes. We must have sausage for supper."

So she finished paring her apples, and spread the fine white cloth on the table, and set out the plates and cups and forks, and then she went to the pantry for the sausages, but, ah, you know where they were!

"Where are my sausages? Naughty pussy; scat," and she sent the house cat outside. "Alas, we shall have nothing but pretzels for supper."

So that was all they had, while the coffee pot sat on the shelf and felt very proud and held his sausages all tightly.

But, listen to what is the end of the story. When it came morning, it was time for the coffee pot to be filled.

"Now I shall be set on the stove, and my sausages will be cooked," said the coffee pot, but that did not come to pass.

"What is the meaning of this?" said the old cook, as she lifted his lid and pulled out the links. She rubbed her eyes.

"The brownie was about while I napped

yesterday afternoon," she said, "and he has been meddling with the coffee pot. It must be well scoured, and it cannot be used for a month after having sausage inside."

So that was all that came of the matter. The coffee pot was scoured and scoured and polished as he had never been cleaned before, and for a month he sat on the shelf with his lid up to let in the air, and holding nothing, while the tea kettle sputtered away:—

"It was against the order of the kitchen, no good could come of it."

Why the Bear Has a Stumpy Tail

ONCE UPON A TIME, in the far away days, when the beasts walked the land, and talked like real people, the bear had a long, beautiful, bushy tail, as fine as the tail of any other creature, and you may be sure he was very proud of it.

One winter day the bear was out traveling, and whom should he meet but Brother Fox, hastening along with a string of fish dangling down his back.

"Ah," said Bruin, "stop a bit, friend; where did you find such fat fish?"

Now, very likely Brother Fox had helped himself to the fish from some one's larder, but he never told the bear; not he.

"It is a secret, about these fish," he said to Bruin; "come close, and I will tell you."

So Bruin went close to Brother Fox, and Brother Fox said:—

"You must go to the river where the ice is thick, make a hole in the ice, sit down with

77

your tail in the hole, and wait for the fish to bite. When your tail smarts, pull it out, quickly. That is the way to fish."

"Oh, is it?" said Bruin. "Well, if you say it is so, it must be true, Brother Fox," and he walked toward the river swinging his tail as he went, and Brother Fox hid behind a tree to laugh up his sleeve, and watch.

Well, poor old Bruin got a stick, and made a hole in the ice. Then he sat down with his long, beautiful, bushy tail in the water and waited, and, oh, it was very cold indeed.

He waited, and waited, and then his tail began to smart. He gave a quick pull to bring up the fish, and, alas, the ice had frozen fast again.

Off came the bear's beautiful, long, bushy tail, and he never was able to put it on again.

And that is why the bear has a short, stumpy tail, because he tried to fish, as Brother Fox told him to, through the ice.

How the Fox Played Herdsman

ONCE UPON A TIME there was a little old woman who had a farm of her very own with sheep, and cows, and swine. But the little old woman was so busy making butter and minding the dairy that she had no time to look after the herds.

One fine morning she started out to hire a herdsman. Now she had not gone very far when she met a bear.

"Whither away, Goody?" asked Bruin of the little old woman.

"Oh, I am off to engage a herdsman for my farm," said Goody in reply.

"Why not hire me, Goody?" asked Bruin.

"Can you call the flocks at evening?" asked the little old woman.

"You should just hear me," said Bruin, and he called in a very loud and gruff voice, "OW, OW."

"No, no, I won't have you," said the little old woman as soon as she heard his gruff voice, and off she went on her way.

She had not gone a day's journey farther when she met a wolf.

"Whither away, Goody?" asked the wolf of the little old woman.

"Oh, I am off to engage a herdsman for my farm," said Goody.

"Why not hire me, Goody?" asked the wolf.

"Can you call the flocks at evening?" asked the little old woman.

"You should just hear me," said the wolf, and he called in a shrill voice, "UH, UH."

"No, no," said the little old woman as soon as she heard that, and off she went on her way.

But before the end of another day's journey, whom should the little old woman meet but Brother Fox, sitting beside a blackberry bush, and sunning himself.

"Whither away, Goody?" asked Brother Fox.

"Oh, I am off to engage a herdsman for my farm," said Goody in reply.

"Why not hire me, Goody?" said Brother Fox.

"Can you call the flocks at evening?" asked the little old woman.

"Ah, you should hear me," said Brother Fox. He opened his mouth very wide, and sang in a sweet voice:—

"Tum-ti-ti, tum-ti-ti-tra-la-la."

"You will do very well," said the little old woman, quite carried away with the fox's sweet singing. "You shall come home with me, and be my herdsman."

Things went very well for a little while at the farm. Early each morning Brother Fox led the sheep, and the cows, and the swine to pasture, and at night he led them home again, and locked the barn, and bolted the pigpen.

But, somehow, after a week, the flocks and the herds seemed smaller each night when the little old woman went out to make the rounds of the farm.

"Where is the small, black pig?" she asked of Brother Fox.

"Loitering in the meadow," said Brother Fox, wiping his mouth with his paw.

"Where is the old ram?" asked the little old woman.

"He stops behind at the brook," said Brother Fox, turning his head away that Goody might not see him laughing.

So Goody went back to the dairy, and she wondered and wondered what made the flocks grow smaller.

At last she had churned enough butter to make a fine cake and she went out to the poultry roost for eggs with which to enrich it.

Alas, such a hubbub, and cackling, and fussing did she find.

The cock stood on the pump, crying loudly, "Cock-a-doodle-do."

The hens ran about cackling, and out of their midst walked Brother Fox with a chicken over his back, and his hat full of eggs.

And as he went along he sang to all the poultry yard: —

> "Tum-ti-ti, Tum-ti-ti,
> Tum, tum, ti,
> Old Goody's herdsman,
> Sly Reynard am I."

"Well, it's certainly a very poor herdsman you are," cried the little old woman. "Where is the small, black pig? Where is the old ram?"

She ran after Brother Fox, who dropped his eggs and broke every one, and tipped over the churn as he passed the dairy. The little old woman picked up the dasher, and would have beaten Brother Fox, but he was too quick for her, and reached the woods, with a drop of cream on the tip end of his tail.

So the little old woman learned what had become of her herds, and Brother Fox was never able to get that cream from off his tail, and the tip end has been white ever since he played at being a herdsman.

The Little Girl Who Wanted the Stars

ONCE UPON A TIME there was a child who wanted all the stars in the sky to play with, and she cried for them from morning till night. One day, she started out by herself to see if she could find them.

She went far, far away, and then farther still, until she came to a mill wheel, creaking and grinding away.

"Good day to you," said the child to the mill wheel; "I want all the stars in the sky to play with. Have you seen any near here?"

"Ah, yes," said the old mill wheel, "every night they shine in my face from the pond until I cannot sleep. Jump into the pond, little girl, and you will find them."

So the child jumped into the pond and swam about, but she could not find any stars. She swam until she came to the brooklet, and to the brooklet she said:—

"Good day, Brooklet. I want all the stars in

the sky to play with. Have you seen any near here?"

"Ah, yes," said the brooklet, "they glint on my bank at night until I cannot sleep. Paddle about, little girl, and you will find them."

So the child paddled about in the brooklet, but she could not find any stars. Then she climbed up the bank, and sat down in the meadow to dry. Now it was a fairy meadow, and when it came night, out scampered the Good Folk to dance on the green.

"Good evening, Good Folk," said the child, "I want all the stars in the sky to play with. Have you seen any near here?"

"Ah, yes, we have," said the Good Folk, "they glisten in the grass in the night time. Come and dance with us, little girl, and you will find as many stars as you like."

So the child danced all night with the Good Folk, but not a star could she find. When it came morning the Good Folk danced away to hide, but they said as they left:—

"Ask Four Feet to carry you to No Feet. Ask No Feet to take you to the stairs without steps. Then climb, and climb up the stairs without steps, and you will find the stars in the sky."

The child thought that this was all very strange. She wandered about, not knowing

They came to a glistening arch in the middle of
the sea.

which way to go, until at last she came upon a little pony, standing, saddled and bridled, in the woods.

"Good day, Four Feet," said the child, "will you carry me to No Feet?"

"I wait for the Good Folk's bidding," said the pony.

"It is from the Good Folk that I come," said the child.

"Then jump upon my back," said Four Feet.

Away they galloped, over field and meadow, until they came at last to the sea.

"I can take you no farther," said Four Feet.

The child looked out over the sea, and in the middle she saw an arch of beautiful colors. It glinted and glistened in the sunlight. It reached to the sky.

And a great fish swam from under the arch, and up to the child.

"Good day, No Feet," said the child, "I want all the stars in the sky to play with. Will you carry me to the stairs without steps, that I may climb up, and get the stars?"

"I wait for the Good Folk's bidding," said No Feet.

"It is from the Good Folk that I come," said the child.

"Then jump on my back," said No Feet.

So No Feet swam, and swam, with the child

upon his back, until they were far from the shore. They came to a glistening arch in the middle of the sea.

"I can go no farther with you," said No Feet, "here are the stairs without steps."

So the child jumped from No Feet's back, and tried to climb up the rainbow, but as fast as she took one step, she slipped back, splash, into the sea.

She tried, and she tried, but it was no use at all. She could not climb up to the sky. So, after a while, she called No Feet, and he took her to the shore of the sea again, and she went home to her mother. She had found out that the stars are too far away for a child to reach, and she never cried for them again.

Why the Field Mouse Is Little

ONCE UPON A TIME, before there were any big folks, or any real houses in the world, the little First Man, and the little First Woman lived in a tiny lodge on the banks of a big river. They were the only people in the whole world, and they were so very, very small, not any larger than your finger.

They ate wild gooseberries, and twin berries, and black caps. One berry made a very fine meal for them.

The little First Woman took very good care of the little First Man. She made him a beautiful green bow and arrow from a blade of grass with which he could hunt crickets and grasshoppers. From the skin of a humming bird she made him a most beautiful hunting coat all embroidered and jeweled with bits of gay shells and shining particles of sand.

One day the little First Man was out hunting and he grew very weary, wading through the deep grass, so he laid him down beneath a clover leaf and fell fast asleep. A storm came up, and the thunder roared and the lightning flashed, but it did not waken the little First Man. Then the sun shone, warm, as it does in hot countries, and the little First Man awoke. Alas, where was his gay little hunting coat? The rain had soaked it, and the sun had scorched it, and it had fallen to pieces, and dropped quite off the little First Man.

Then he was very angry and he shook his fist at the great sun. "It is all your fault," he cried. "I will pull you down from the sky."

He went home and told the little First Woman, who cried many tears when she thought of all the stitches she had put into the coat. And the little First Woman stamped her little foot at the sun, and she, too, said it should stay up in the sky no longer. The sun should be pulled down.

The next thing was to arrange how to do it. They were such small people, and the sun was so great and so far away. But they began plaiting a long rope of grass that should be long enough to catch the sun, and after they had worked for many moons, the rope was quite long.

Then they could not carry it, because it made such a heavy coil; so the little First Man tried to think of one of the beasts who could help him, and he decided that the Field Mouse would be the most willing.

In those far away days, the Field Mouse was much larger than he is now, as large as a buffalo. The little First Man found the Field Mouse asleep under a tree, and he had great trouble awaking him, but the Field Mouse was very obliging. He took the coil of rope upon his back, allowed the two little people to sit, one on each ear, and they started away to find the woods where the sun first drops down in the evening.

It was a journey of many moons, and most tiresome. There were many rivers to be forded, and at each one the Field Mouse was obliged to take one end of the rope in his mouth, and swim over with it. Then he would coil it up, and go back for the little First Man, and the little First Woman.

But at last they came to some deep, dark woods where the beasts, the elk, the hedgehog, and the others, assured them the great sun dropped down every night, last of all.

Then the little First Man climbed to the tops of the trees, making slip knots of the rope, and fastening it to the branches until he had made a huge net, larger than any fish net you ever saw. When it was done, they all hid to wait for evening, and to see what would happen.

Such a terrible thing happened! Lower, and lower, fell the sun toward the woods that he always touched the last thing at night. And before he could stop himself—down into the little First Man's net he dropped, and he could not get out.

No one had ever thought what would happen if the sun were caught. Of course everything was set on fire. The trees smoked, and the grasses blazed. The little First Man and the little First Woman started running toward home as fast as ever they could, because of all the mischief they had done. The elk had his antlers scorched. The hedgehog was obliged to dance to keep his feet from burning, and the other beasts crowded around Field Mouse.

"Good, kind Field Mouse," they cried, "will you not set the sun free? Your teeth are sharp. Gnaw the rope, and loose him, we pray of you."

So the Field Mouse, who was always most good natured, climbed to the top of a tree and gnawed the rope with his sharp teeth, although it was very hot and uncomfortable for him. Gnaw, gnaw, and at last the sun was loose. With a bound it jumped to the sky, and there it has stayed ever since.

But what do you think happened to the Field Mouse? The heat melted him down to the size he is now, and that is the reason the Field Mouse is so very little.